Mildred Childress

This book belongs to

Esmerelda

The Silly Goose

Esmerelda
The Silly Goose

By

Mildred Tickfer Childress

Illustrated by
Susan Johnson Zipperer

Wynden *Books*
an imprint of **Canmore Press**

Canmore Press, P.O. Box 510794, Melbourne Beach, FL 32951-0794

Published 2004

Printed in China on archival paper

Illustrations by Susan Johnson Zipperer

© Book and cover design by Lyn Cope-Robinson, Canmore Press

Contents and decorative fonts are Adobe Jenson Pro® designed by Robert Slimbach. Adobe Jenson Pro is based on Renaissance typefaces drawn by Nicolas Jenson and Ludovico degli Arrighi.

Esmerelda, the Silly Goose was inspired by one white goose who lived among a flock of Canadian geese in Allegan County, Michigan. Observations of her summer behavior and her particularly distressing calls when the wild flock migrated inspired this story.

Library of Congress Cataloging-in-Publication Data

Childress, Mildred Tickfer, 1931-
  Esmerelda the silly goose / by Mildred Tickfer Childress ; illustrated by Susan Johnson Zipperer.
      p. cm.
  Summary: Craving adventure, a silly barnyard goose flies off with a herd of wild Canadian geese going north for the summer.
  ISBN 1-887774-17-3 (alk. paper)
  [1. Canada goose--Fiction. 2. Geese--Fiction.] I. Zipperer, Susan Johnson, ill. II. Title.

PZ7.C44125Es 2004
[Fic]--dc22
                                              2004016849

ISBN 1-887774-17-3 $11.95

Dedication

To all of my children and grandchildren

Contents

Chapter One
Esmerelda is Restless

There was no question about it. Esmerelda was a silly goose. After all, didn't she have a perfectly lovely home? She lived in a barnyard with her ma and pa and her two brothers and three sisters. (Of course it was a long waddle to the pond beyond the woods.) There was plenty to eat. The farmer's wife put out cracked corn every morning. Esmerelda and her family had to share with four chickens and a duck but there was always enough for everyone.

But Esmerelda was unhappy. She was tired of sharing the cracked corn. She didn't like the long waddle to the pond and she didn't think the greens in the farmer's strawberry patch were particularly tasty.

She hadn't talked about how unhappy she was. But she often stood with her head tipped first to one side and then tipped to the other side. She looked like she was thinking very hard. She was thinking about running away.

Esmerelda didn't really know where she'd go. She'd never been away from the farm but she was sure there was an exciting world filled with adventure just waiting for her to explore it.

Then one beautiful spring morning as Esmerelda and her family were eating weeds in the farmer's strawberry patch some of that excitement flew into her life. Nine gray geese flapped noisily overhead. They sailed over the woods and there was much honking and splashing. Esmerelda knew they were swimming in her pond. Esmerelda had never seen a wild goose before. Her ma had told her there were such things and said they didn't really have a home. They wandered from place to place looking for food and pretty much had to look out for themselves

Esmerelda inched closer and closer to the edge of the strawberry patch. Her ma and pa were still busily pulling weeds and no one seemed to notice that she was not. She just had to get a better look at these gray geese.

There! She was in the woods now. No one had

missed her in the strawberry patch. She waddled faster and faster to the edge of the pond. Yes, there they were. Oh, weren't they beautiful! Some of them were in the pond splashing water onto their feathers and rubbing them with their bills. Others were in the sunny spot of grass beside the pond. They were hunkered down like they were resting. Esmerelda wondered where they had come from and where they were going. She wanted to talk with them but she was shy and none of them had even noticed her.

Just then one of the gray geese that had been washing his feathers swam over toward Esmerelda. She began to preen her feathers and pretended not to notice him.

Chapter Two
Adventure Calls

The gray goose strutted up on the grass beside Esmerelda. He flapped his wings very hard. Esmerelda knew he was drying his wings. But she also knew he was trying to get her attention. She continued to preen her feathers.

"You come here often?" the gray goose finally asked.

"Every day." Esmerelda replied. "I live on the farm just beyond the woods." There was a long pause.

"Where do you live?" Immediately Esmerelda wanted to bite her wing tips in embarrassment. She knew. Her Mother had told her. Wild geese didn't have homes.

"I mean, er, where did you come from—this morning?" Esmerelda stammered. She knew she was just making things worse.

"We've been traveling for several days," the gray goose replied. He didn't seem to notice her confusion. "We spent the winter far to the South of here but it was time to come back. When the long warm summer days come we like to be here in the Northland."

"Here?" Esmerelda asked. "Here?" She looked around the pond. It really wasn't all that big. And with ma and pa and her brothers and sisters there were already nine geese and sometimes the duck came for a swim, too. If these nine wild geese moved in it could be mighty crowded by fall.

No, not here, here," the gray goose giggled. "We just stopped for a drink and to rest our wings. We'll be moving on soon.

"Do you have much farther to go?" Esmerelda was genuinely interested.

"No, actually, it's only about an hour flying time from here."

"What will you do when you get there?" Esmerelda was full of questions.

Now the gray goose seemed embarrassed. "Well, it is springtime and that means nesting and starting a family."

"Oh, of course," Esmerelda started preening her feathers again. She knew that.

Why did she keep asking embarrassing questions? And then she did it again.

"Which one is your mate?" she asked, looking toward the other gray geese?

Now the gray goose was preening. "Er, I don't have a mate yet. Perhaps when we get to the big pond—," he left his sentence unfinished.

Esmerelda's silly goose heart began to pound faster. She waddled slowly to the edge of the water and sailed gracefully off toward the center of the pond. She needed time to think. But she turned her head ever so slightly first this way and then that. She wanted to see if the gray goose was still watching her.

She wondered if a handsome gray goose such as he was would ever consider a plain white barnyard goose for a mate. She was planning to leave here anyhow. This was a marvelous opportunity to broaden her horizons. She shifted her course and circled back toward the gray goose who was still watching her from the edge of the pond.

Esmerelda was sure he was very interested in her. She neared the edge of the pond. She spread her toes and dragged her feet to slow her approach.

"How long will you be staying here?" Esmerelda wanted to know how much time she had to plan her next move.

"We'll be moving again this afternoon. We're really not crowding you. There are only nine of us."

Esmerelda thought he sounded a bit huffy.

"I wasn't trying to get rid of you, I was only curious." She tried to sound as pleasant as she could.

"I've never met a wild goose before," she added.

The gray goose relaxed his long stiff neck and began nipping at the soft grass.

Suddenly very hungry, Esmerelda joined him on the bank. She nibbled daintily hoping the gray goose would be impressed with her manners. She kept her head down and seemed to be paying a lot of attention to her diet but she was very aware of where the gray goose was and what he was doing.

"If they are going to move on this afternoon," Esmerelda was thinking, "I could just hang around here until they leave. Maybe I could follow them for a little way—just to see what it's like to be a wild goose. If it only takes an hour to get where they're going that can't be that far away. Why, I can always come back to ma and pa if I want to. But then, why would I want to? Pulling weeds in the garden is such a bore. Life with the wild geese would be so exciting and I never have to go back to the farm again if I like the wild life."

Chapter Three
Decision Time

Several of the other gray geese had joined them on the bank and were also foraging on the soft grass. One of them sidled up to Esmerelda's new friend.

"Nice spot you picked here, Greg."

"Greg—probably short for Gregory," thought Esmerelda. What a fine name—Gregory Goose." Esmerelda was more sure than ever that she wanted to join this wild group. She was willing to follow them wherever they went.

As she grazed, Esmerelda moved ever closer to Gregory Goose. When she felt like she was in a good spot to attract his attention, she made a great display of flapping her wings. A small shower of droplets made it obvious she was just trying to dry off. But she was pleased when Greg looked up.

"Do you think—um—er—" Esmerelda didn't quite know how to ask this. "When you leave here this afternoon could I maybe—," Esmerelda was nervously nibbling her wing tips again. But Greg's head was tipped thoughtfully to one side. She had his full attention. "I'd like to tag along. I'm really tired of this little puddle and pulling weeds in the strawberry patch all day is not very exciting. I think I'm ready to see the world."

Greg didn't say anything for a minute and Esmerelda was sure he was going to laugh at her or tell her she wasn't welcome to join their group.

"Can you do it?" he asked.

"Of course, I'm nearly an adult. I don't need permission." Esmerelda sounded quite huffy.

"No, I mean CAN you? Have your wings been clipped?"

Esmerelda spread her wings and inspected them carefully. "No, I don't think so."

Greg smiled at her seriousness. "You'd know if they

had been. Sometimes farmers clip the wings of their barnyard birds so they can't do just what you want to do—fly away."

"Oh!" Esmerelda was a little embarrassed by her ignorance. The farmer had probably been counting on her youth and her attachment to her ma and pa to keep her on the farm. She supposed the cracked corn his wife threw out every morning was supposed to help, too.

But Esmerelda's silly goose heart was yearning for excitement and she couldn't wait to get started. She hoped the flight would get underway before the barnyard fowl waddled down to the pond for a mid-day swim. It would be easier to leave if she didn't have to explain anything to ma and pa.

"Can you fly? I mean how far have you ever gone?" Greg was trying not to insult her, Esmerelda was sure.

"Well, it's such a short walk through the woods I haven't needed to fly much. But I have practiced some. See, I've been thinking of leaving here for some time," Esmerelda confessed. "You said it would only be an hour or so. I think I can make that."

Gregory Goose had been walking around her and looking her over very carefully.

She was young and strong. She was not heavy like

many barnyard geese and she surely had her mind set on doing this. He supposed it wouldn't hurt to let her come.

"We'll be leaving soon," he said and strutted away like a king who had just bestowed a favor on a peasant.

Chapter Four
Flight to Freedom

E smerelda's heart was already flying. She began to think about those short practice flights and tried to remember everything she had learned. She didn't want to look clumsy or even worse not be able to take off.

Suddenly she realized that all of the gray geese were in the water. Quickly she slipped into the pond and paddled out to where they were. They were all babbling noisily. Esmerelda listened carefully to the instructions and the flight plan. Greg was to be the leader and she was to have third position back on his right. She wasn't happy about being so far back from him but she decided not to make an issue of it.

With much honking and flapping and splashing the nine gray geese and silly Esmerelda took to the air. They climbed quickly to clear the trees at the edge of the pond. Esmerelda stole one quick look backwards. Ma and pa and the other barnyard fowl were just coming out of the woods. Esmerelda had no time for a further look. She didn't even call or wave goodbye.

Flying was much harder work than Esmerelda remembered. She had to concentrate very hard to keep up with the others.

They had continued to climb so that they were a comfortable distance above even the tallest trees and they all began to fall into their appointed positions in the formation. As Esmerelda slid into her position behind Carolyn, she suddenly felt a lift that made it easier for her. With every flap of Carolyn's wings there was an air spill around the tip of her wings, which created an upward current of air. By flying just above and behind her, Esmerelda could save quite a bit of effort. Esmerelda was tempted to just sail along on this current but she knew Harold, the bird behind her in the number four position, was depending on her wing flaps to provide the lift for him.

There was a lot of conversation among the geese as they sped along.

They were all excited at being near the end of a very long flight. They honked and called out to each other, good-naturedly teasing one another.

After a while Harold moved up to the head of the vee and Greg slipped into the number two position on the left. Even though he was closer to her he was quiet. Esmerelda figured he was probably just resting.

Being the leader of the vee took quite a bit of energy. Esmerelda could understand why the leadership changed so often. She was grateful that they were protecting her by not asking her to fly in that position.

Esmerelda was beginning to grow very weary. "Greg said it would only be an hour," she fretted to herself. "It's been several hours, already, I'm sure." She was just beginning to work herself up to a fine stage of unpleasantness when the increased honking of the other geese prompted her to look down.

Spreading out below her was a marvelous lake with indistinct edges blended by cattails and tall grass into long broad fingers of marshland. Esmerelda caught her breath at the beauty and bigness.

The geese broke formation as they all swooped at once to come to a splashing halt. Again they called noisily to one another, congratulating themselves on a successful flight.

Esmerelda bobbed about on the water. She spread the webs of her feet as wide as she could. They felt all cramped from having been tucked up underneath her tail for so long. Greg came sailing up beside her.

"Welcome home," he grinned. "We made pretty good time. We slowed the pace a little so you could stay with us and still it only took an hour and a half."

"It seemed much longer," sighed Esmerelda. She was grateful for the consideration.

Chapter Five
The Beautiful Summer

Esmerelda thought she had never been so happy. This was absolutely the most beautiful spot she had ever seen. She paddled around in a complete circle three times just trying to take it all in. This was more than a big pond. It was a lake. The water was clear but contained all of the kinds of grasses and tiny snails that geese find incredibly delicious.

Most of the gray geese were already hungrily stuffing themselves. The stopover at Esmerelda's pond had been more of a rest stop than a lunch break. It had been several days since there had been time for leisurely eating their fill. They were scooping whole mouthfuls of lake water and lifting their heads to let the water drain from their beaks leaving behind the tasty bits of plankton and algae.

Gregory Goose began to maneuver Esmerelda around to meet the rest of the flock. She had announced her travel plans so close to departure there hadn't been time for proper introductions and getting acquainted.

Harold and Carolyn, who had flown near her, were an older couple. They had been coming here for the summer for five years. Two of their daughters, Ann and Agnes, and their mates, Bill and Tom, were here, too.

They hoped a couple of their other children would be among later arriving flocks.

Frank and Eleanor were newcomers to this group. They had only been together since last spring. They had three teen-aged daughters that were traveling with another group. They also were expected to arrive at any time. Eleanor was quite anxious for them to meet Esmerelda as she was sure that they were all her age.

Esmerelda nodded politely but thought she'd rather they didn't show up. Without them, her competition for Greg's attention was zero.

Bill and Ann and Tom and Agnes were already scouting the marshland for nesting sites. This was their first season together and they couldn't wait to begin building their nests.

Esmerelda was thrilled with her new home and her new friends. Every day there were new arrivals.

Frank and Eleanor's daughters arrived each in the company of a young male goose and they were all busily looking for nesting sites.

The days flew by quickly and Esmerelda kept hoping Greg would be interested in getting their nest started. But he hadn't said a word about it. Esmerelda thought they should get started soon. After all, some of the others already had several eggs in their nests. Finally when she couldn't stand to wait any longer Esmerelda brought it up herself.

"Have you thought about where the nest should be?" She asked shyly.

"What nest?" Greg looked surprised.

"Our nest, silly," Esmerelda was nibbling her wing tips again.

"No, Esmerelda, you are the silly one," Greg replied gently.

"I said you could tag along for the excitement but I didn't say anything about a permanent arrangement."

Esmerelda was more than embarrassed. She was humiliated. At first she was angry with Greg and she paddled away as fast as she could.

"What a mess," she thought. "Here I am, who knows how far from home and this goose I came with wants nothing to do with me." But after a while she began to cool off and do some sensible thinking.

Greg really hadn't promised her anything. She couldn't blame him. She had been the one who asked to come. If he chose a different mate or no mate at all it meant nothing to her.

Esmerelda settled in for a summer of enjoyment. There were a number of single geese from other flocks that were always available for exploring and playing water games. They would take short flights following a waterway that emptied into the lake. There was much merriment and calling back and forth. They practiced takeoffs and landings but none of them ever got the hang of starting from dry ground.

There were a few casualties, of course. One morning as Esmerelda was gliding toward one of her favorite eating spots she heard an uproar behind her. Turning quickly she paddled over to where several more geese were gathering about Tom and Agnes who were hastily urging their goslings out of the water. "What's all the fuss about?" Esmerelda asked Greg who was on the outside of the group.

"I haven't figured it out yet," Greg replied. "Something about how awful it is and no one is safe anymore."

"Look!" Esmerelda pointed with her beak. "Didn't they have five goslings yesterday?"

"Yes, I'm sure of it but you're right; there are only four, now."

"Poor Agnes," thought Esmerelda as she pushed her way through the noisy crowd to find out what had happened.

"A snapping turtle!" moaned Agnes when Esmerelda finally reached her.

"We were out for our second swim. You remember we were out yesterday, too. The children were all doing so well, staying right in a line, just so. Tom was in front and I was in the rear keeping an eye out for stragglers.

"It sounds so safe," murmured Esmerelda.

"And then the turtle grabbed the middle one by the leg and pulled him under so quickly he didn't even have time to peep. The turtle dove, and they were both gone as quick as a flash. Oh, my poor baby."

Esmerelda was truly sorry for Agnes and Tom. But she knew the tender little Gosling had undoubtedly been a tasty dinner for the big turtle. Esmerelda knew she was too big to be attacked by a turtle but she was more careful all the same.

Chapter Six
Practice Flights Begin

One morning as Esmerelda slid into the water and paddled onto the lake for her morning feed, she realized that she was all alone. There was not a gray goose to be seen anywhere. Esmerelda tried not to panic but where was everyone? "Greg! Ann! Bill! Agnes…" She began calling the names of her friends as she paddled back and forth across the lake. A terrible sense of loneliness came over her.

It was so quiet she could hear the ripples behind her as her webbed feet made tight little circles under her. Fan the toes and sweep down, fold the webbing, draw up, and push forward to fan the toes again. Over and over she repeated this process without even thinking about it. Her mind was on Greg and the others.

Where were they? Had they abandoned her? Now her calls for them were more like cries. Her voice grew hoarse. She continued to scan the horizon looking for any movement that might be a sign of their return.

Hours went by. Esmerelda became acutely aware of her surroundings. She noticed that the leaves of the oaks had yellowed and the maples were fire red.

"Funny. Had they been like that yesterday?" she wondered.

In the late afternoon Esmerelda waddled up out of the lake and made her way to a neighboring corn field. She had found this place on one of her exploring trips and had made many return visits. It reminded her of the cracked corn the farmer's wife had thrown out for her back home. She wondered how things were back there. Did ma and pa still miss her? The weeding work was probably pretty much the same. Even though she remembered how boring it had seemed she thought of it from this distance almost fondly.

It was nearly dusk when Esmerelda heard them. Honking and flapping the gray geese had returned and were splashing down into the lake. Esmerelda waddled out of the cornfield and hurried back to the lake.

"Where have you all been?" Esmerelda asked Greg. She was quite irritated.

"We've been on a practice flight." Greg had a maddening way of not noticing that she was upset.

"A practice flight? What are you practicing for?" Esmerelda could hear the anxiety in her voice but she couldn't help it.

"Our trip South." Greg was being quite short with her, she thought.

"Well, why didn't you tell me? Shouldn't I be practicing, too?" she sputtered.

"Oh, Esmerelda, you are such a silly goose. Too many trips to that cornfield have fattened your barnyard goose frame. You could never make a flight like we're planning. You can hardly get above the tree line anymore. I'm afraid this trip is not for you." Greg sailed elegantly off paying no attention to the fact that he had seriously wounded Esmerelda's feelings.

Chapter Seven
The Longest Practice Flight

Esmerelda wanted to cry. Greg had made it clear she was not really an accepted member of the flock of gray geese But more than that, he had pointed out quite bluntly that he thought she was fat. Esmerelda paddled furiously to the other side of the lake to a shallow place in a shady cove. She waddled ashore and then standing at the edge of the water, she studied her reflection. She turned sideways and tipped her head first one way and then the other. Greg was right. She had definitely lost her girlish figure. She had matured and grown quite plump.

Esmerelda was pleased to realize how grown-up she looked. Why, she looked just like her ma. On the other hand being so heavy was going to be a problem for her in the near future. But Esmerelda was such a silly goose she chose not to think about that just now and she waddled off to a nearby pasture for something more to eat.

The next morning Esmerelda was quite pleased to find that all of the grey geese were still there. They hadn't gone sneaking off on another silly practice flight. That all seemed so foolish to Esmerelda. Why did they need to practice, anyway? In spite of Greg's unkind remarks she was quite sure she could still fly. She remembered perfectly well how they got here. She had flown then, hadn't she? When it came time to go she'd show him. He didn't need to think he was so smart.

For several days everything was pretty much as it had been all summer. The goslings were all teenagers now and really anxious to act grown-up, so of course they only wanted to talk about the big trip. There was much talk among the older ones about being with other family members and friends once they reached the South. Esmerelda was pretty quiet during these discussions, but she really believed when the time came she would go, too.

Of course, when the others talked about their families she thought about ma and pa and the others. Sometimes she almost missed them but this life was so exciting she really wasn't ready to go back to the farm.

There were other practice flights, and each time Esmerelda felt a little panicky when she realized they had gone without her. Those were long lonely days and she paddled aimlessly about the lake calling for the others to return.

By mid-October there was a definite chill in the air. The lake was getting colder, too. Most of the maple leaves were on the ground now and the oak leaves, though clinging tightly to the branches, were withered and brown. The gray geese had been gone for three days on their most recent "practice flight". This was the longest they had ever been gone. As much as Esmerelda wanted to believe that Greg would not really leave without saying goodbye, her hopes became fainter each day.

Chapter Eight
Esmerelda Goes It Alone

After several days Esmerelda had to face the reality that the gray geese would not be returning. Now, what was she going to do? She could just stay here and wait for their return in the Spring. But even silly Esmerelda knew that was not the answer.

She wasn't a snow goose. In fact, as long as she was facing reality, she wasn't even a wild goose. She was just a plain barnyard goose and she had been away from her natural environment for several months. Esmerelda needed to go home.

She needed to be about it rather quickly, too. The

weather had become colder and her already heavy body had further protected itself by adding more fat. It was impossible for her to get into the air for even a short flight unless she started in the water. The area of open water was smaller every day as new fingers of ice formed, grabbing the lake away from her. Yes, she must go soon.

The first thing she needed to consider was direction. She remembered when they had come here they approached the narrow end of the lake first.

If she started from there and just kept going in that direction that should do it, shouldn't it? Greg and the others had headed out that way, too. That must be right.

How long had it taken her to get here from the farm? Several hours, she thought. Of course, that had been all flying time. And flying with a flock was much different from going it alone. She couldn't waste any more precious time thinking about it. It was time to go.

She swam toward the narrow end of the lake, getting as close as she could. She had to leave plenty of room between herself and the extending ice for takeoff. Her first try at lift-off was unsuccessful. She was quite stiff from the cold, but she knew it was essential for her survival to leave the lake. She circled around, aimed herself south. Esmerelda flapped her wings very fast. This time she made it! She was up! She was flying— not too high, actually. But she was above the treetops. Esmerelda felt a thrill. She could do it!

Already her wings could feel the strain of her heavier body. Her determination forced her to keep moving. She tried not to think about how tired she was and just keep her wings flapping. Over and over she repeated the motions. Fatigue was her enemy.

She missed the support of the others. She hadn't realized just how important that had been. Not only had it made flying easier but the challenge of staying up with the rest had extended her strength. Going it alone, she had to depend on her own raw courage.

Getting out of the lake and up into the air had been very hard. Staying up there was even harder. Esmerelda was really straining to keep going. She knew it hadn't been this hard for her when she came North. She supposed it had something to do with the new full figured look she had developed.

She also knew it had been much easier when she had been part of a flock. Working together helped all of them. She wondered if the flock missed her. Sadly she realized they probably didn't. At least, they didn't need her like she needed them. They might miss her quick jokes and friendly ways. But, their trip South would go just fine without her.

Esmerelda was feeling quite sorry for herself. She knew it was her own fault she was in this mess. She was the one who had decided to leave the safety of the farm. And Greg had warned her of the danger of overeating. Still, she had slipped off to the cornfield again and again.

She could feel her heart pounding and knew her strength was going. Gradually she dropped lower and lower. She skimmed the top of a small tree and then a bush and then she was down. She didn't like landing on the ground. There was no cushion.

There was no way to glide to a stop but there was no water to be seen and Esmerelda simply could go no further.

She waddled into some tall grass for cover and hunkered down out of sight to rest.

Chapter Nine
Alone and Friendless

Esmerelda woke with a start. She had been sleeping quite soundly for some time. The sun had already passed the midpoint of the sky. She knew it must be well into the afternoon. Her stomach was reminding her there had been no breakfast and no lunch either, for that matter.

"It certainly was silly of me to go flying off without at least one last visit to the cornfield," Esmerelda scolded herself.

"On the other hand," she reasoned, "it would only have made the flying that much harder.

But, it was certainly time to eat now. Esmerelda

waddled out of her grassy hiding place. She found herself in a clearing. There were bushes not far away.

She was headed that direction so she decided to have a closer look. Maybe there would be some berries.

Esmerelda nibbled on some grass as she moved toward the bushes. It was dry and prickly. She wished for some of the tender green weeds from the farmer's garden back home.

When she got to the bushes she was disappointed again. They were bare of leaves. There were no berries. And there were lots of sharp thorns.

Esmerelda was miserable. She was hungry and very lonely. She wasn't sure how far she was from home. She wasn't even sure she was headed in the right direction.

Suddenly there was a flurry of wings. Several large birds sailed into the clearing behind her. They were talking noisily to each other. Esmerelda's spirits brightened immediately.

Peeking cautiously around a bush Esmerelda could see that they, too, were looking for something to eat. She watched as they lifted first one foot then the other. She thought the dry grass must feel prickly to them too.

Esmerelda suddenly felt quite shy. She had been

wanting company more than anything. But now she didn't know quite how to go about making friends. On the other hand she was even more afraid they would leave as quickly as they had come. She did not want to be alone again.

Stepping boldly out of the bushes she greeted them.

"There really isn't much that tastes good, is there?" It wasn't brilliant conversation but she thought it would do for an opener.

"What are you doing here?" the plump turkey was somewhat unpleasant, Esmerelda thought.

"I'm looking about for a bit of a bite to eat," she responded pleasantly.

"Well, aren't you a silly goose! Most of your kind headed South weeks ago." The other turkeys seemed quite content to let this fat hen do all the talking.

"I'm headed south." Esmerelda said defensively.

"By yourself?" This time the Tom spoke up. He sounded more kind, Esmerelda thought.

"Well, I really don't have much farther to go." Esmerelda hoped she sounded more confident than she felt.

"Will you turkeys stay around here for the winter?"

"Of course," snapped the fat one again. "And you needn't be having any fancy ideas of joining up with us."

Esmerelda was nervously nibbling her wing tips. What had she done to upset this turkey so much?

"I had no intention," she stammered, "of barging in where I'm not wanted."

"Thomasina, can't you keep a civil tongue in your head? You haven't been the least bit polite. Can't you see that this goose is lost and lonely?" The Tom turkey seemed to be quite friendly.

"Well," sniffed Thomasina as she strutted away, "I just think she'd be happier with her own kind."

Esmerelda wondered what Thomasina meant, but decided not to ask. She really had been more comfortable with the wild geese, and most comfortable of all, back on the farm where life had been more predictable. She was trying to get back there.

More and more she was very sorry she had ever left.

"Is there any water near here?" Esmerelda called after the retreating turkeys.

She knew they needed water for drinking even if they didn't care about swimming.

"River's that way," gobbled the Tom who also seemed to be more indifferent now. He nodded in the direction Esmerelda thought she ought to be traveling.

Esmerelda was quite relieved to part company with the turkeys. She waddled off in the direction indicated to find water. She glanced back and the turkeys were gone from sight. Esmerelda envied their strong legs that could help them walk and even run long distances. She needed to move as fast as she could. She wanted to find the river before dark.

Chapter Ten
Dark Night in the Big Woods

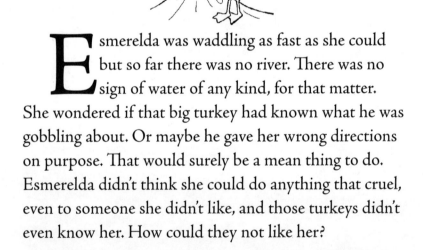

Esmerelda was waddling as fast as she could but so far there was no river. There was no sign of water of any kind, for that matter. She wondered if that big turkey had known what he was gobbling about. Or maybe he gave her wrong directions on purpose. That would surely be a mean thing to do. Esmerelda didn't think she could do anything that cruel, even to someone she didn't like, and those turkeys didn't even know her. How could they not like her?

It was getting dark. Esmerelda could hardly see where she was going. She was in the woods. The trees were close together and very tall. They were mostly pine trees so there were a lot of pine cones on the ground.

That made it slow going because the pine cones hurt Esmerelda's big webbed feet.

It was hard to keep going in the right direction because of the trees. It was impossible to walk in a straight line. She tried veering to the right for one tree and then veering to the left for the next. She hoped that would balance things out so she wouldn't get too far off course.

She kept her head down looking for pine cones. Then, thump, she ran right into a tree trunk. Esmerelda knew it was too dark to try to go any farther. She might just as well give up and stop for the night.

She hunkered down and tucked her head under her wing. Esmerelda didn't fall asleep right away. There were too many strange noises. The wind had started to blow and somewhere overhead two branches were rubbing together with a terrible scraping sound.

"Whooo."

Esmerelda shivered. That was a new sound. She burrowed her head further under her wing. She didn't want to hear any more of that noise and she surely didn't want to see where it was coming from. And then there it was again.

"Whooo."

It was enough to give Esmerelda duck-bumps. She didn't believe she'd ever been so frightened. She didn't know where that sound was coming from but she was sure it was something alive. She decided to be very still. She wished she were some color other than white so she wouldn't be so visible. It would even help if she weren't so fat.

At last, Esmerelda slipped into an uneasy sleep. And as she slept, she dreamed.

In her dream she was walking through the little woods near the pond back home. She was almost to the farmer's garden. She was coming out of the woods now and could see her ma and pa and the other barnyard fowl busily eating weeds.

"Ma!" she called. Her ma raised her head and stretched out her long neck.

"Whoo?" She acted as if she didn't even know Esmerelda.

"It's me, Esmerelda, don't you know me?"

"Whoo?" repeated her ma.

"Pa," Esmerelda was desperate, "don't you know me either?"

"Whoo?" was pa's reply.

A feeling of panic filled Esmerelda's chest and her little heart was racing.

She woke with a start to realize it had all been a dream. Only an owl, somewhere high above her, was real.

Shifting her weight from one foot to the other Esmerelda risked a peek. Slowly she lifted her wing and opened one eye. The darkness was beginning to pale. She could see dark shapes that were surely the trees. Esmerelda knew it would soon be morning. She was anxious to be on her way home.

Chapter Eleven
A Fox and A Hound

There were pink streaks in the sky and the trees were clearly visible. Esmerelda stretched her long neck and gave her wings a couple of flaps.

She was drying the dew that had settled on her overnight. How she wished she were at home in the barnyard coop with ma and pa and the others.

The closer she got to home the stronger were her memories of the good life there. Thoughts of Greg and the other grey geese were quickly fading.

In fact, when she thought of them at all, she was overcome with embarrassment at how foolish she had been. To even think she could live the wild life only proved what a silly goose she was.

By now Esmerelda could see the bushes and tree branches plainly and she knew it was time to get moving. Just as she stepped out from under the tree where she had slept she saw out of the corner of her eye something moving. Turning her head quickly she caught a glimpse of a red fox. He slipped behind a bush and waited.

Esmerelda was sure she didn't want to hang around to get acquainted. She remembered all too well her pa telling how his brother had been caught by a fox. Esmerelda began to run. She needed to find a clearing so she could get into the air. She knew the fox was not far behind her.

The brush and sticks on the ground tore at her webbed feet. She couldn't think about that now. She was going as fast as she could but with her heavy frame it was more waddle than run.

At last Esmerelda could hear water. She crashed through a line of bushes, leaving some feathers behind, and slid down the mud bank into the river.

The water was cold but Esmerelda was able to move more swiftly now. This was her element. Her feet were paddling furiously. She was starting to feel safe when she noticed the fox slipping along the edge of the river just ahead of her.

With great effort Esmerelda flapped her wings and lifted her heavy body into the air. Her fear of the fox sent a wave of energy through her frame. Up, up she went, over the tops of the trees. Her head was pointed again in the direction of home. At least, she hoped she had the direction right. She wished she had paid more attention when she was flying with the gray geese.

"I guess," Esmerelda sighed to herself, "If I had been paying attention to directions I would never have left home."

Again the weight of her body was too much for her wings. She began to drop lower and lower. She knew she would have to land, and looked down for a good spot.

She had left the river and was over farmland. She was looking for soft ground. A barking dog gave her another surge of energy. She sailed up over a row of trees before gliding down and landing with a running thump in a pasture.

Chapter Twelve
Home At Last

Esmerelda continued to waddle in the direction she had been flying. The going was easier here. There were some fences she had to go around. But for the most part she could stay on course.

Esmerelda was almost exhausted. She had had enough exercise and excitement to quite wear her out. She began to think seriously about giving up. But the thought of never seeing ma and pa and the others gave her a tight pain in her chest. She knew she would have to keep looking for home as long as she could keep moving.

Suddenly she realized that she was in familiar surroundings. Why, here was her pond! It was frozen solid but she recognized the shape. And over there beyond the trees, she knew, was the barnyard.

Esmerelda waddled even faster now. She could hardly wait to see ma and pa and the others. Coming out of the woods into the strawberry patch she couldn't see anyone.

The farmer and his wife would be in the house and the geese and duck in the coop, she reasoned.

She waddled up the plank and through the door into the coop. There was a welcoming flurry of excitement. Suddenly all the bravery and energy it had taken to get her home drained away. She felt quite shy and very tired.

"Where have you been?" sputtered ma.

"I thought we'd never see you again," sighed pa. "It's good to see you safe at home again".

For a while Esmerelda was too tired to talk. She just wanted to rest. Then she was more than happy to take her turn at the pan of cracked corn and the water dish. The younger geese and the duck were full of questions.

"Where did you go?"

"What did you do?"

"What did you see?"

Esmerelda told them, slowly at first but with growing excitement all about her adventures. She included many references to herself as a silly goose so that none of them would be so foolish to try what she had done.

That evening when the farmer's wife came with the cracked corn she recognized Esmerelda immediately. She called the farmer and he came to see for himself. He inspected her carefully, gently removing some sharp sticks that were caught in her wings.

"Yes, I'm quite sure it's Esmerelda." he said to his wife. "I'll clip her wings tomorrow. That should keep her safely at home from now on."

"Oh," Esmerelda thought. "I'm not going anywhere ever again."

But the farmer clipped her wings all the same. While he was about it, he clipped the wings of all the geese and the duck.

Esmerelda was very happy to be snug in the coop all the long cold winter.

Finally spring had erased the last of the snow and ice. It was time to return to the strawberry patch.

Esmerelda was busily at work but she heard them. Honking noisily overhead, the gray geese were winging north again. Esmerelda didn't even look up.

This was such a comfortable safe place to be. She didn't know how she could ever have been such a silly goose.

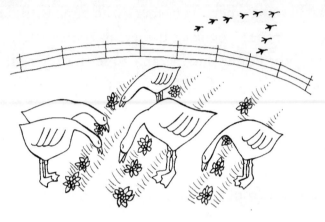

The End

About the Story

The author spends summers at Sandy Pines, a RV Recreational Park, in Allegan County, Michigan. Sandy Pines surrounds Lake Monterey frequented by Canadian geese and numerous other wild life that live throughout the area near Little Rabbit River and Swan Lake.

One summer, one white domestic goose lived among the wild Canadian geese. No one seemed to know where she came from or how she got there. In late fall when the gray geese began their practice flights, the white goose would paddle from one end of the lake to the other calling plaintively.

Eventually the wild flock migrated and the white goose was left alone. She continued her lonely circuits on the lake and her cries grew more and more pitiful. At times it seemed the goose even grew hoarse. It was the observation of this incident that gave birth to the Esmerelda story.

About the Author

Mildred Tickfer Childress was born in southwestern Michigan and raised on a small fruit farm near Watervliet. She notes that she has had a love affair with words and stories all of her life.

Her first book, *Healing the Hurt*, for teens whose parents are divorcing, was written for neighbor children who came to her for counseling when they were hurting. As a Psychiatric nurse, she has had numerous articles published in professional and Christian journals. But with her busy career in nursing, and raising her family, she had no time to capture her spun-from-real-life stories for younger children onto paper until she retired.

She was married for forty-four years and is the mother of three adult children. She remarried after the death of her first husband, and she and her present husband have thirteen children, twenty-one grandchildren, and five great-grandchildren.

She is a resident of Indian Harbour Beach, Florida, and finds tremendous enjoyment and inspiration in walking on the beach and wading in the Atlantic Ocean.

About the Illustrator

Susan Johnson Zipperer was born in Greenville, North Carolina, grew up in southern Virginia, and attended Florida State University. She presently lives in Indian Harbour Beach, Florida with her husband and three children.

Esmerelda, the' Silly Goose' is her first children's book. A potter by trade, Susan Johnson Zipperer creates functional stoneware and porcelain pieces—exhibiting that ability with her elusively simple line renderings of Esmerelda. Her large murals grace many homes in the area, as well as the children's wing of her church.

Spending the day at the beach with her family observing coastal wild life is a favorite activity. She is also very involved in Children's Ministry exploring values and art with the very young.